An I Can Read Book™

Minnie and Moo
meet
FRANKENSWINE

by
DENYS
CAZET

HarperCollinsPublishers

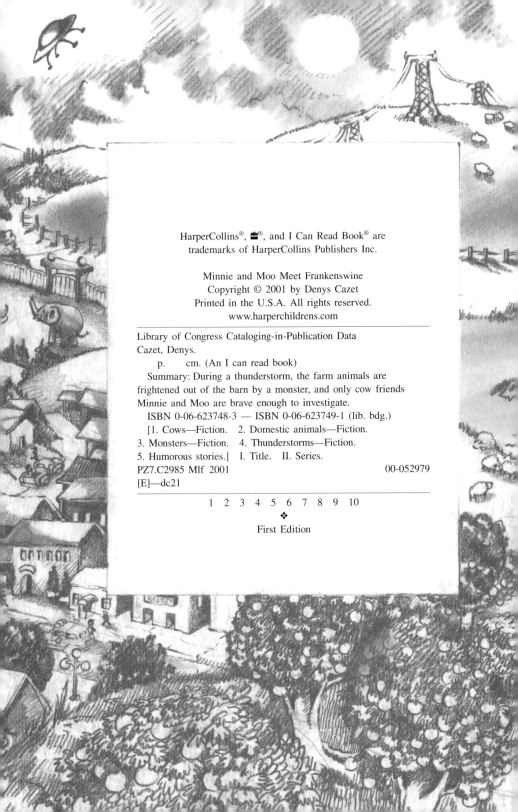

Minnie and Moo Meet Frankenswine
Copyright © 2001 by Denys Cazet
Printed in the U.S.A. All rights reserved.
www.harperchildrens.com

Library of Congress Cataloging-in-Publication Data
Cazet, Denys.
   p.   cm. (An I can read book)
   Summary: During a thunderstorm, the farm animals are
frightened out of the barn by a monster, and only cow friends
Minnie and Moo are brave enough to investigate.
   ISBN 0-06-623748-3 — ISBN 0-06-623749-1 (lib. bdg.)
   [1. Cows—Fiction.   2. Domestic animals—Fiction.
3. Monsters—Fiction.   4. Thunderstorms—Fiction.
5. Humorous stories.]   I. Title.   II. Series.
PZ7.C2985 Mlf 2001   00-052979
[E]—dc21

        1   2   3   4   5   6   7   8   9   10
                         ❖
                   First Edition

Things in the Night

It was a dark, dark night

on top of the dark, dark hill.

Lightning flashed.

Thunder rumbled.

Dry leaves rustled in the dark.

Moo wrapped her blanket

tightly around her.

She stared into the night.

Something moved.

"Minnie," she whispered.

Minnie snored.

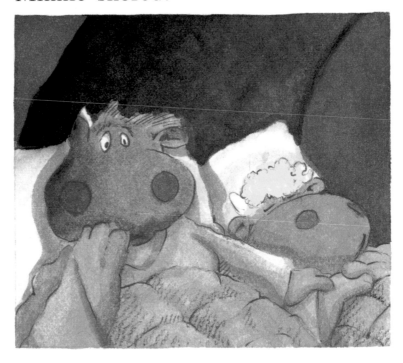

Moo shook her gently.

"Minnie," she said. "Are you awake?"

Minnie sat up. "What?"

"Are you awake?" Moo asked.

"I am now, Moo," said Minnie.

"Why did you wake me up?"

Moo pointed into the dark.

"Something is out there," she said.

Lightning crashed.

Thunder boomed.

There was a scream in the night.

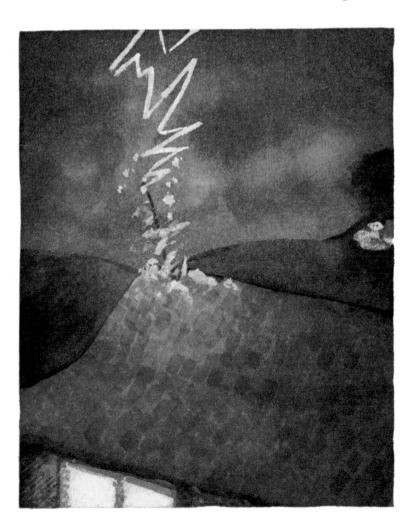

Monster in the Barn

Minnie and Moo jumped up.

"What was that?" Minnie asked.

"The barn," said Moo.

"Something's glowing in the window."

Suddenly,

the barn doors flew open

and all the animals ran out.

The animals ran up the hill.

"MONSTER IN THE BARN!"

shouted the rooster.

"Every chicken for himself!"

"Save us!" begged the sheep.

"Poor Olga," a pig wept.

"Gone," cried another.

"Gone, gone, gone," said Zeke.

"Like a turkey through the corn,"

said Zack.

The Holsteins puffed up the hill.

"Bea, Madge," said Moo.

"What happened?"

"Can't talk," Madge wheezed.

"Monster," gasped Bea, as they ran

toward the farmer's house.

Monster on the Hill

The moon peeked from behind

a black cloud.

"Where did they go?" Moo asked.

Minnie said, "They're hiding

behind the farmer's house."

Moo glanced back at the barn.

The window was dark.

"Minnie . . . this is the kind of night
that curdles your milk," Moo said.
A bat flew past her face.
"Ohhh!" she gulped.
"Maybe we should go
with Bea and Madge."
"Moo . . ." said Minnie.

The wind moaned softly
in the old oak tree.
Moo looked up
into the dark branches.

"What was that?" Moo whispered.

"Moo—" said Minnie.

"This is the kind of night," said Moo,

"when monsters sit in old oak trees

waiting to jump on kind

and decent cows—"

"Moo—" said Minnie.

"This is the kind of night," said Moo,

"when monsters glow in the dark and—"

"MOO!" Minnie blurted.

"WHAT?" Moo shouted.

Minnie put her arm around Moo.

"You were having a thinking fit,"

Minnie said gently.

"Oh," said Moo. "Sorry.

Sometimes a cow can't help it."

Moo said,

"This is the kind of night when—"

Lightning flashed.

Thunder boomed.

A light went on in the farmer's house.

There was a scream in the night.

Monster in the Farmhouse

The animals ran around the corner of the farmhouse.

They leaped over the picket fence and ran back up the hill.

"THE MONSTER'S

IN THE FARMHOUSE!"

shouted the rooster.

"We saw the light!" yelled a sheep.

"It ate the farmer!" said another.

"And the farmer's wife!" said a third.

"And my cousin, Olga," cried a pig.

The Holsteins huffed

and puffed up the hill.

They sat down under the old oak tree.

"Is the monster coming?" asked Bea.

"No," said Moo. "All I see

are Zeke and Zack."

"Too bad," wheezed Madge.

"If it's going to eat us,

I hope it starts with my feet.

They're killing me!"

Zeke and Zack trotted over

to Minnie and Moo.

"The monster threw the farmer's leg

out the window," said Zeke.

"What?" said Moo.

"It hit me on the head," said Zack.

"See the lump?"

Minnie looked at Zack's head.

"Which lump?" she asked.

"The new one," said Zack.

Zeke threw something on the ground.

"What is that?" asked Moo.

"The farmer's leg," said Zack.

The Farmer's Leg

Everyone stood in a circle

around the farmer's leg.

Madge poked it with a stick.

"He sure was skinny," she said.

Just then, the light went off

in the farmhouse.

Moo saw it.

"Minnie," she said, softly.

"Doesn't the farmer get up

and go to the bathroom

at this time every night?"

Minnie looked at the farmhouse

and then at the farmer's leg.

She picked it up. The animals gasped.

"You are right, Moo.

But tonight, he was a little slow

in getting there!"

"How fast can you walk

after someone throws your leg

out the window?" said the rooster.

"Maybe he hopped," said Bea.

"He didn't hop," said Minnie.

"He walked . . . because *this* . . .

is *not* his leg!"

"But if that isn't the farmer's leg,"

said Madge, "then . . . whose is it?"

"Everyone check your legs,"
ordered Bea.
"It's not mine," said Zeke.
"I've got mine," said Zack.
"Not ours," said the sheep.

"That's the farmer's leg,"

said the rooster. "There's his toe."

"That's a very big toe," said Moo.

"It must be swollen," said the rooster.

"This is a branch from the apple tree

in the farmer's yard," said Minnie.

"And this 'toe' is an apple!"

"But what about the monster?"
Bea asked.

"THERE!" shouted the rooster.

The Rooster's Story

Something glowed in the barn window.

"MONSTER IN THE BARN!"

shouted the rooster. "It's back!

It ate the farmer and his wife,

and now it wants us!"

"Poor Olga," cried a pig.

"She just came for a visit and—"

"Will you forget about Olga!"
said the rooster. "Olga's bacon."

"Ohhh!" The pig wept.

Minnie glared at the rooster.

She didn't like him.

"*You* saw the monster?" she said.

"It was huge," said the rooster.

"It had horns and six-inch fangs.
Its nose was blue."

"It glowed in the dark," he said,

"and sparks shot out of its bottom!"

"Sparks?" said Moo.

"Sparks!" said the rooster.

"Like on the Fourth of July,

sparklers, 'Piccolo Petes,'

stuff like that!"

"Did anyone *else* see the monster?"

Minnie asked.

The animals shook their heads.

"Hey!" said the rooster.

"I have the eyes of an eagle.

I know a monster when I see one!"

Minnie rolled her eyes.

"If you cows are so brave,

why don't you go down there

and see for yourselves!"

the rooster said.

Moo looked at Minnie.

Minnie looked at Moo.

"Let's think about this," said Moo.

"No more thinking," said Minnie.

"It's time for doing!"

The Monster

Minnie and Moo

tiptoed down the hill.

They stopped at the barn.

Minnie put her ear to the door.

"Do you hear anything?" Moo asked.

"Yes!" whispered Minnie,

"and it's coming this way."

Moo gulped.

"Get ready to open the doors,"
said Minnie. "Here we go.
One . . . two . . . THREE!"
They threw open the doors.
The barn was dark
and empty,
except . . .
for a small pig
who glowed in the dark.

"IT'S FRANKENSWINE!!!"

screamed the rooster.

"Run for your lives!" shouted Zeke.

"Head for the hills!" shouted Zack.

"FRANKENSWINE'S MONSTER!"

cried the rooster.

He dashed back up the hill.

The chickens followed,

clucking and flapping behind him.

They hid under the old oak tree.

Then it was quiet.

The glowing pig looked
at Minnie and Moo.

"Who are you?" asked Minnie.

"Olga," said the little pig.

Olga's Story

The animals gathered around Olga.

"What happened?" asked Moo.

Olga took a deep breath.

"Well," she said, "I'm not sure.

I was sleeping by that big machine.

There was a flash of light,

and I lit up like a Christmas tree."

"That machine is the electric milker,"
said Minnie.

"Lightning must have struck it!"

"It curled my hair," said Olga.

Minnie fluffed Olga's hair.

"It looks nice on you," said Moo.

"Yes, yes," said Minnie. "But we're going to have to do something about that bald spot in the back."

"How about rubbing a little shoe polish on it?" said Moo.

"Oh," said Olga, touching her head.

"We will give your hair a nice trim in the morning," said Minnie.

Olga wandered off with the other pigs.

Minnie and Moo

looked out the barn window.

It began to rain.

Lightning lit up the night sky.

"I think I see the rooster sitting

under the old oak tree on the hill,"

said Moo.

Minnie picked up a blanket.

"Don't be silly, Moo.

Even the rooster

isn't dumb enough to sit under a tree

in a thunderstorm."

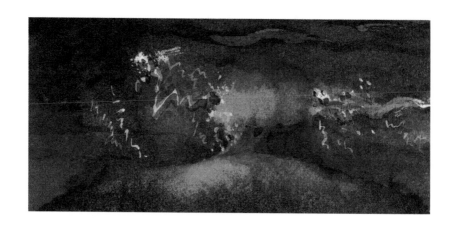

Lightning flashed.

Thunder rumbled.

There was a scream in the night.